THE FORGOTTEN PRINCESS

F. H. MICKEL

ILLUSTRATED BY NICOLE GUIDO

With love
To Jeanne, my muse and co-pilot

This Book Belongs to:

_____

Long ago in a European land was a beautiful kingdom. Each spring, it's fields would fill with daffodils, and the queen's ladies-in-waiting would come to gather flowers for the palace. The flowers considered it a great honor to be chosen. This would give them a chance to show off their beautiful colors and aromas inside the walls of the palace. When the flowers bloomed again the next year, those who had been chosen had special status. They would tell stories of what they had seen inside the palace: the beautiful vases in which they were held, their places of honor on banquet tables, and all the latest gossip of the queen and her court. On and on they would go as the new flowers listened excitedly and hoped that someday they too would be chosen.

In a distant corner of one of the fields stood a lonely flower in what had once been the private garden of the beloved Princess Faith. Princess Faith had ruled the kingdom with great love and kindness for her subjects. Life had been good for them all. In time, however, Princess Faith had married a prince from a distant land and moved away. Years passed and her private garden was left untended by the current queen who had always resented Princess Faith's popularity with the people, and really didn't care about flowers anyway. Finally, only one flower remained in a garden overrun by weeds. The other flowers made fun of her because she had never been picked, for no lady-in-waiting would dare pick a flower from Princess Faith's garden, lest the queen might find out. They had learned it was best not to irritate the queen.

Perhaps the lonely wait would not have been so hard if the other flowers had been kinder to her. But they mockingly called her "Princess" because no matter how many times she was left unpicked, she always held her head high.

"Who does she think she is anyway?" huffed one.

"She's been living with the weeds for so long she is beginning to look like one," snorted another.

"Why would anyone pick her when *I* am so much more lovely?" boasted a third.

"Well, I heard the queen was going to have that old garden dug up and burned," said one daffodil knowingly.

Princess trembled as she wondered if this could possibly be true. She thought to her self: *"I know they are beautiful, but I have many fine qualities also. Besides, it's a wonderful spring day and the sun feels just as warm on my face no matter what they say."*

And so it went, year after year, always unpicked, always hopeful . . . until one year dozens of the queen's helpers came to gather flowers in their aprons. As they talked among themselves, the flowers listened carefully.

"We will need thousands of flowers if the queen's orders are to be carried out," said one.

"Yes," said another, "I heard this will be the grandest ball ever thrown in the kingdom."

"I was told that things are not going well for the queen," said a maid who worked in the queen's chambers. "She has spent all her money and must make an alliance to survive. She has invited the most powerful prince in Europe to be the guest of honor."

Princess was so happy listening to all this. Surely she would be picked this year with such a dire need for flowers. She lifted her head proudly and waited . . . but no one came.

As the sun set, she looked across the fields and could not see another flower left unpicked. Since there was no one there to see, she started to cry.

"What is wrong with me? Can I be that horrible? Now I know I will never be picked," she cried and cried.

The next day she could see all the carriages arriving for the ball and hear all the excitement within the walls of the palace.

"I guess I'll hear all about it next year from the flowers that are now inside," she thought. Even though she knew it would be difficult to be the only flower left unpicked, Princess was still anxious to hear about the festivities. She could hear the music late into the night, until finally, she cried herself to sleep.

When Princess awoke in the morning she felt lonelier than ever. Even though the other daffodils were mean to her, being alone was even worse. She was trying not to feel sorry for herself. It was, after all, a beautiful day, and slowly, the warm sun put a smile on her face. Just then, she heard the gates of the palace open. This was not unusual, but what followed was. For there was the queen herself walking with a beautiful woman. Normally, the queen was not one for fresh air. In fact, Princess had never before seen the queen. She was fascinated to watch the procession as the queen and her companion were followed by a continuous stream of attendants flowing from the gates.

Her fascination turned to fear, however, when she realized they were walking very much in her direction. Could they be coming to dig up and burn the garden as she had heard earlier?

Soon she could hear the queen's voice.

"I know it's out here somewhere, my lady," she was saying, "although I can't imagine what interest it could hold."

"Well, it's such a glorious day for a walk; let's wander around a bit," said the woman.

Princess could now see that the woman with the queen must herself be very important; yet, there was something in her manner that was reassuring. This woman could mean no harm. Princess stretched her head as high as she could above the weeds to get a better look . . ., and just as she did, she could see the woman's eyes gazing directly at her.

"Over here," the woman cried. "That must be it," she said as she hurried towards Princess.

"Don't be ridiculous," said the queen. "It's probably just an old weed. It's certainly a poor excuse for a daffodil."

"It certainly is," said the woman, "because, my lady, that is a tulip."

Princess was confused. She had always thought she was a daffodil, although not a very good one. She did not know what to make of being a tulip. The woman approached Princess and gently put a sweet-smelling finger to one of her petals and explained to the queen.

"You see, my grandmother was Princess Faith, and when she left your kingdom, she brought with her a reminder of her most cherished memories from home . . . her garden. With bulbs taken from this very spot she started a garden for her new home in Holland. Over the years, they grew and grew and became exceedingly valuable. As a little girl, I remember her telling me that as beautiful as her garden was, it could never be as beautiful as the one she left behind.

She always dreamed of returning to see her garden one day. But I am glad she is not here to see how you have let it go untended. If you had nurtured this garden, you would still be rich; but instead, you cannot repay the money you borrowed from my husband, and at this very moment, he is foreclosing on all of your possessions."

"And, you, my treasure," said the woman as she gently dug Princess from the ground and placed her in a golden vase, "are coming with me to meet all of your grandchildren."

The queen was flabbergasted! "But. . . but. . . but" was all she could say.

Princess felt as though she would faint from happiness; not because she was valuable, but because for the first time, she was truly seen and loved for what she was. . ., not for what others thought she should be.

The next spring when the daffodils bloomed again, they talked endlessly about the events after the grand ball. How wonderfully different the new queen had been. How Princess really was a princess with millions of subjects. They all agreed that they had always loved Princess and knew she was special. And as they looked over the fields, they saw for the first time, not just daffodils, but tulips, and many other flowers. All different, yet all beautiful. Somehow, they all felt even better and more lovely because they were part of something bigger than themselves. For generations until this day, they all live together in harmony and tell the story of Princess.

The End

"The Earth laughs in flowers"
Ralph Waldo Emerson

A special thanks to Nicole Guido who brought
The Forgotten Princess to life through her art.

CPSIA information can be obtained at www.ICGtesting.com
Printed in the USA
LVIW01n0938070816
499395LV00020B/236